The Chronicles of

Narnia

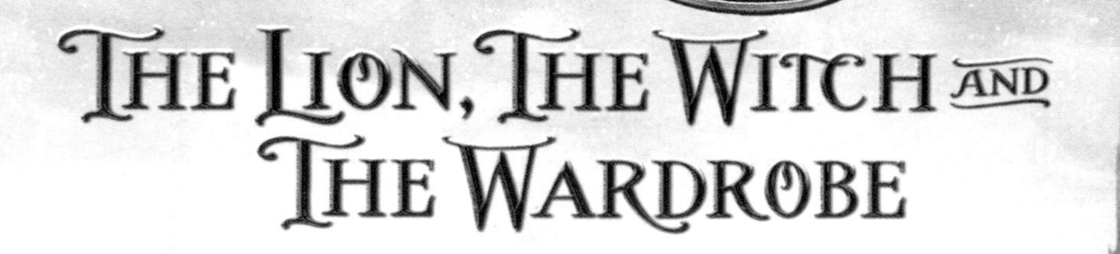

Edmund and the White Witch

Adapted by Scout Driggs

Illustrated by Justin Sweet

Based on the screenplay by Ann Peacock and Andrew Adamson
and Christopher Markus & Stephen McFeely

Based on the book by C. S. Lewis

Directed by Andrew Adamson

An Imprint of HarperCollins*Publishers*

WALT DISNEY PICTURES AND WALDEN MEDIA PRESENT "THE CHRONICLES OF NARNIA: THE LION, THE WITCH AND THE WARDROBE" BASED ON THE BOOK BY C.S. LEWIS
A MARK JOHNSON PRODUCTION AN ANDREW ADAMSON FILM MUSIC COMPOSED BY HARRY GREGSON-WILLIAMS COSTUME DESIGNER ISIS MUSSENDEN EDITED BY SIM EVAN-JONES PRODUCTION DESIGNER ROGER FORD
DIRECTOR OF PHOTOGRAPHY DONALD M. McALPINE, ASC, ACS CO-PRODUCER DOUGLAS GRESHAM EXECUTIVE PRODUCERS ANDREW ADAMSON PERRY MOORE
WALDEN MEDIA SCREENPLAY BY ANN PEACOCK AND ANDREW ADAMSON AND CHRISTOPHER MARKUS & STEPHEN McFEELY PRODUCED BY MARK JOHNSON PHILIP STEUER DIRECTED BY ANDREW ADAMSON Walt Disney Pictures

Narnia.com

The Lion, the Witch and the Wardrobe: Edmund and the White Witch

Library of Congress catalog card number: 2004117935

Printed in the United States of America. For information address HarperCollins Children's Books, a division of HarperCollins Publishers, 1350 Avenue of the Americas, New York, NY 10019.

Book design by Rick Farley

1 2 3 4 5 6 7 8 9 10

❖

First Edition

Edmund Pevensie wasn't very happy. His older siblings, Peter and Susan, always bossed him around. And his little sister, Lucy, got all the attention. When Lucy said there was a secret land just behind the coats in the wardrobe, Edmund didn't believe her. But he decided to follow her, just in case.

Edmund had barely gotten past the last bulky coat when he felt an icy breeze. He spun around, but everywhere he looked, he saw only snow and trees. And before he could call for Lucy, a sleigh pulled by reindeer came into view.

In the sleigh was a lady who was both beautiful and terrible at the same time. She was wrapped in white fur and held a golden wand in her hand. On the top of her head sat a many-pronged crown. She was the White Witch, Queen of Narnia.

"And how, pray, did you come to enter Narnia?" the White Witch demanded.

"I'm not sure," answered the frightened boy. "I was just following my sister and . . ."

But the White Witch wasn't listening to Edmund. She was thinking about how to get rid of him and his sister, and any other Humans who came to Narnia. She knew Humans were the only creatures who could end her evil rule over the land.

"You're the sort of boy I could see as a Prince of Narnia one day," the Witch said with an evil smile.

Really? wondered Edmund, feeling quite proud of himself.

Next, the White Witch raised a copper vial and let one drop of liquid fall into the snow. A shimmery box appeared, filled with an enchanted treat called Turkish Delight! It was Edmund's favorite candy in the world. But the Witch already knew that. It was all part of her evil plan.

"Come to my castle as soon as you can," the Witch said. "But of course you must bring your family—you'll need servants." And with an evil grin, the Queen swept off in her sleigh.

Edmund chuckled. He liked the idea of being in charge. He'd never have to take orders from his family again—he would be the Prince of Narnia!

A few days later, Edmund was back in the wardrobe, but this time he wasn't alone. His three siblings, Peter, Susan and Lucy, had gone into the wardrobe with him.

While Peter and Susan were looking around in wonder at the snowy woods, a voice came from the trees. *"Pssst, pssst, pssst!"*

The children looked over to see a friendly Beaver signaling to them. He quickly led the group through the forest to his dam, where they would be safe.

Mr. Beaver brought the children to his cozy home. While his wife gave them some food, he explained that Narnia was a dangerous place, ruled by an evil Queen. "She put Narnia under a snowy curse so it's always winter," Mr. Beaver told them. "And she turns any creature who gets in her way into stone."

But Edmund didn't bother to listen to what Mr. Beaver was saying. Ever since he had gotten back to Narnia, all he could think about was going to see the Queen again. He could hardly wait to become a Prince and order his brother and sisters around.

Edmund sneaked out into the night while his siblings were listening to Mr. Beaver's long stories.

It was a long way to the castle, and his feet were getting stuck in the deep snow. But he kept going, thinking about all the wonderful things waiting for him once he arrived at the Witch's house.

When Edmund entered the courtyard, he saw a horrible sight. There were stone creatures everywhere—their faces frozen in fear.

Edmund was scared. But he tried to be brave. Soon he would be Prince of this entire land, and Princes are known to be brave.

"Follow me," said a voice from the dark.

It was Maugrim, a fierce Wolf who was Captain of the White Witch's Secret Police. Maugrim led Edmund to a vast hall made entirely of ice.

Poor Edmund. When Maugrim finally took him to the White Witch, she yelled, "How dare you come alone!" and threw him into the dungeon. She had never meant to make him a Prince. She just wanted to capture him and his siblings.

Meanwhile, Peter, Susan and Lucy tried to find someone to rescue Edmund. That's when they met Aslan, the *real* King of Narnia. He was a great and kind Lion, more powerful than the White Witch.

Aslan sent his brave Centaurs to rescue Edmund. When the White Witch turned her back, they untied Edmund and put the Dwarf who had been guarding him in his place! Then the Centaurs rushed Edmund through the forest to Aslan's camp.

But the White Witch was not far behind. When she got to the camp, Aslan agreed to let her take him instead of Edmund. It was a great sacrifice, but Aslan kept it a secret from Edmund and his siblings. They only knew that Edmund was safe, and they were very glad to see one another again.

But the adventure doesn't end there. You see, the children joined Aslan's great army. And Edmund helped lead the troops into battle and defeat the White Witch. He and his siblings became Kings and Queens of Narnia and ruled for many happy years.